Sweet Revenge

Sweet Revenge

Robin and Chris Lawrie

Illustrated by
Robin Lawrie

Acknowledgements
The authors and publishers would like to thank
Julia Francis, Hereford Diocesan Deaf Church
lay co-chaplain, for her help with the sign language
in the *Chain Gang* books.

Published by Evans Brothers Limited
2A Portman Mansions
Chiltern Street
London W1U 6NR

© Robin and Christine Lawrie

First published 2001

The authors assert their moral right to be identified as the
authors of this work in accordance with the Copyright, Designs
and Patents Act, 1988.

Printed in Hong Kong

British Library Cataloguing in Publication data.
Lawrie, Robin
  Sweet Revenge. – (The Chain Gang)
  1. Slam Duncan (Fictitious character) – Juvenile fiction
  2. All terrain cycling – Juvenile fiction 3. Adventure stories
  4. Children's stories
  I. Title II. Lawrie, Chris
  823.9'14[J]

ISBN 0 237 52264 0

We have been taking part in the Sword in the Stump Challenge. This is a series of off-road races which is supposed to promote good sportsmanship between young riders. The last two will be downhill races. The rider who scores most points in the series can try to pull the sword out of the stump. The sword appeared at the bottom of the course just before the series started.

* I'm Andy. (Andy is deaf and uses sign language.)

It was Thursday, the day before the downhill race weekend was due to start. We were in the village buying food for camping. My old foes, Stick and Spanner, were up a ladder, painting an old folks' home. They were doing community service. Last year, they had been arrested for trying to spoil a car rally. They blamed me for getting them caught.

SPLAT!

Friday morning: practice day on Westridge. The Tuer Racing team van containing my arch rival, "Punk" Tuer, and his new mechanics, had arrived early. Stick was showing off on his motor bike.

It was fun watching him make a fool of himself.

But we had things to do.

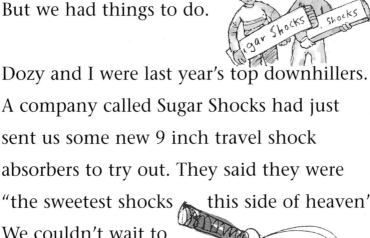

Dozy and I were last year's top downhillers.
A company called Sugar Shocks had just
sent us some new 9 inch travel shock
absorbers to try out. They said they were
"the sweetest shocks this side of heaven".
We couldn't wait to
get in some practice,
but first we had
to make sure
we'd fitted them
properly.

Downhill bike racing is a race against the clock on a rocky, rooty, off-road course about a mile long. A good time for the Westridge course is 2 minutes 30 seconds.
Thanks to the Sugar Shocks, Dozy and I were doing it in 2 minutes 10 seconds. It was like riding on a cloud!

Later that morning, I overheard Punk talking to Stick and Spanner.

Slam's and Dozy's new shocks are amazing. We've got to have a closer look.

It can be arranged.

We had decided to stay on the course campsite and started to set up our tent beside Dozy's dad's van. He lets us use it as race headquarters. Dozy fills it with so much hi-tech gear that there is only enough room for him to sleep inside.

Fionn camped with the other girls.

We weren't
happy when the
Tuers' van moved
into the space next to us. Stick and
Spanner started unpacking their tools.

13

So we packed
up the tent
and headed to the
top of Westridge.
Dozy came too.

14

15

10:00 p.m. We had set up camp and were trying to sleep.

2:00 a.m. Still awake.

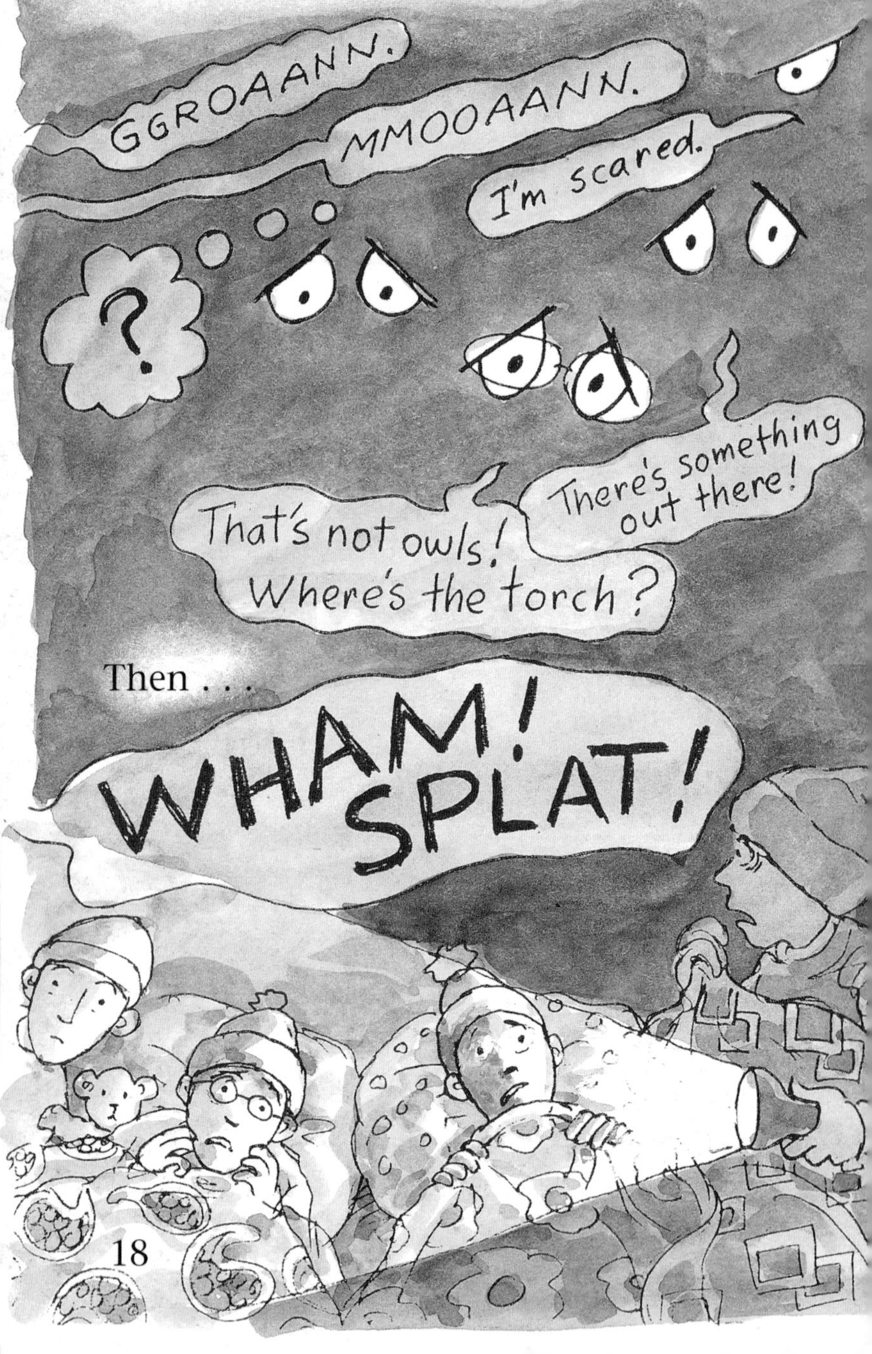

We dared to peep out and saw . . .

So we crept back.

We decided to go back down the hill and have a look inside the Tuers' van.

21

I sat on Andy's shoulders to get a look
inside. I could see Stick and Spanner
taking the pressure cartridges
out of Dozy's shocks.
Then Punk's dog
started to bark
and we had to leg it.

Hmmm!

In practice next
morning, Punk
was really flying!

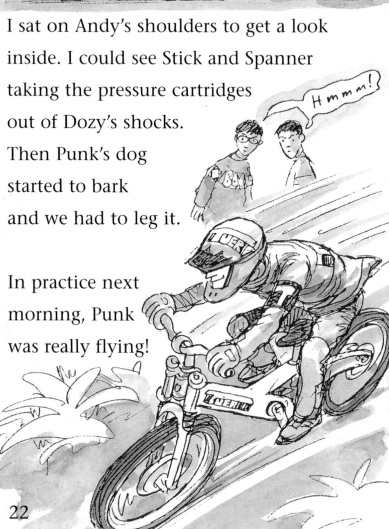

And during the race, his two runs
were the fastest of the day.

A hundred points for Punk.
Andy also did well, coming
third, and Larry, fifth. No
points for me or Dozy.

Punk's done pretty well,
thanks to the insides of
my shocks.

We're going to
have to sort this.
I have a plan.

23

That night we all squeezed into Dozy's
van. I'd been home and
got my sister's fright wig
and some
make-up.
Fionn went
to work
on me.

Dozy set up
his webcam.
Andy took a cable from it and plugged it
into the satellite dish on the Tuers' van.

He watched Punk
through the skylight,
waiting for him
to turn on the TV,
like he always did.
But tonight he decided to play cards
with his crew. Then,
we saw Andy sign:

1. Punk 2. going to bed. 3. Send 4. text message 5. saying 6. Turn on 7. TV.

Dozy signed back:

Andy looked over the other side of the van.

He signed:

Punk's mobile rang.

0 8 3 1 2 4 9 6 7 5

1. Haven't got 2. number.

So he did!

Next morning,
Dozy's shocks were
outside our tent.
We managed to fit them to his bike

 just before his
first run.
The buzzer went
and he was off!

He was
faster than
he had ever been
through the technical section.

28

He flew over
the jumps, whizzed
through the fast field section,
and crossed the finish line,
in the best time of the day.

Andy came second and, even on my old
shocks, I came third.

When the series points were added up . . .

They decided to pull together.

They felt the sword move.

LOYALTY · FAIR PLAY

They looked at each other,
then at the rest of the gang
and Fionn said:

C'mon, give us a hand.
We wouldn't be here
if it wasn't for you lot.

So we all
took hold
and. . .

SHARING

31